Happy
Christmas
Lulu

To Sue, Nigel and Lucy
with love

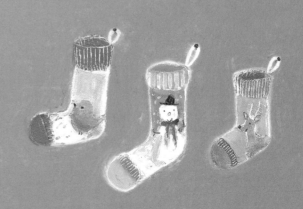

You can also read

Hello Lulu
ISBN 1 84121 728 X

Lulu's Busy Day
ISBN 1 84121 590 2

Happy Birthday Lulu
ISBN 1 84121 618 6

and # Lulu's Holiday
ISBN 1 84121 088 9

ORCHARD BOOKS
96 Leonard Street, London EC2A 4XD
Orchard Books Australia
Unit 31/56 O'Riordan Street, Alexandria NSW 2015
ISBN 1 84121 348 9
First published in Great Britain in 2002
Copyright © Caroline Uff 2002
The right of Caroline Uff to be identified as the author
and the illustrator of this work has been asserted by her in
accordance with the Copyright, Designs and Patents Act, 1988.
A CIP catalogue record for this book is available from the British Library.
10 9 8 7 6 5 4 3 2 1
Printed in Singapore

Happy Christmas Lulu

Caroline Uff

little ORCHARD

Hello
Lulu.

Are you
getting ready
for Christmas?

Glue, glue, stick, stick.

What a lovely
glittery card.
"For my Granny,"
says Lulu.

Time to get the Christmas tree.

It's cold outside.
Wrap up warm,
Lulu.

Brr! Brr!

"Look at our beautiful tree," says Lulu.

Twinkle, twinkle, fairy lights.

Lulu loves her big sister's Christmas play.

"Away in a manger..." sings Lulu with all the other children.

What a lot of shopping bags, Lulu.

Oops! Don't drop them.

Lulu and her big sister
are busy cooking.

Mmm! Those biscuits look delicious.

Hooray, it's Christmas day!

What a lot of presents. And one for Lulu's puppy too.

Woof!

Woof!

Lulu loves
her presents.

Lulu's baby brother loves playing with the paper.

Scrunch! Scrunch!

Yum! Yum! Christmas dinner for everyone.

Happy Christmas Lulu!